Lee and the Box

Written by Catherine Casey
Illustrated by Kelly O'Neill

Collins

Lee sees a box.

Lee thinks it will be fun.

Lee sails in a boat.

He sees a shark.

Lee has a farm with goats.

The ducks quack.

Lee sits on a chair.

Bees buzz in the garden.

Lee bangs and booms.

He sings a song.

At night the doll naps.

The box is fun.

Is it a box?

After reading

Letters and Sounds: Phase 3

Word count: 59

Focus phonemes: /ai/ /ee/ /igh/ /oa/ /oo/ /ar/ /air/

Common exception words: and, the, he, be

Curriculum links: Expressive arts and design

Early learning goals: Reading: use phonic knowledge to decode regular words and read them aloud accurately; read some common irregular words

Developing fluency

- Your child may enjoy hearing you read the book. Emphasise the repeated initial sounds (page 9: **Bees buzz**, page 10: **bangs and booms**).
- Read the left-hand pages while your child reads the right-hand pages. Check they read the common exception words correctly (e.g. **the**).

Phonic practice

- Challenge your child to find a word that contains the /ar/ phoneme on pages 5, 6 and 9.
- Ask them to sound out and blend each word.
  - page 5 sh/ar/k page 6 f/ar/m page 9 g/ar/d/e/n
- Repeat, asking your child to find and read the words that contain:
  - the /ee/ grapheme on page 2 (L/ee, s/ee/s)
  - the /air/ grapheme on page 8 (ch/air).

Extending vocabulary

- Turn to page 7 and point to **quack**. Ask your child what noises other birds make. (e.g. *tweet*, *chirp*, *twitter*, *whistle*)
- Turn to page 9 and point to **buzz**. Ask your child what noises other insects and animals make. (e.g. *moo*, *snort*, *honk*, *squeak*)
- Turn to page 10 and ask your child to think of different words they could use instead of **bangs** or **booms**. (e.g. *clangs*, *crashes*)